Jeff's Job

The Sound of J

by Cecilia Minden and Joanne Meier • illustrated by Bob Ostrom

The Child's World

Published by The Child's World®
1980 Lookout Drive
Mankato, MN 56003-1705
800-599-READ
www.childsworld.com

The Child's World®: Mary Berendes, Publishing Director
The Design Lab: Design and page production

Library of Congress Cataloging-in-Publication Data
Minden, Cecilia.
Jeff's job : the sound of j / by Cecilia Minden and Joanne Meier ; illustrated by Bob Ostrom.
p. cm.
ISBN 978-1-60253-406-3 (library bound : alk. paper)
1. English language–Consonants–Juvenile literature. 2. English language–Phonetics–Juvenile literature 3. Reading–Phonetic method–Juvenile literature. I. Meier, Joanne D. II. Ostrom, Bob. III. Title.
PE1159.M564 2010
[E]–dc22 2010002919

Printed in the United States of America in Mankato, MN.
July 2010
F11538

NOTE TO PARENTS AND EDUCATORS:

The Child's World® has created this series with the goal of exposing children to engaging stories and illustrations that assist in phonics development. The books in the series will help children learn the relationships between the letters of written language and the individual sounds of spoken language. This contact helps children learn to use these relationships to read and write words.

The books in this series follow a similar format. An introductory page, to be read by an adult, introduces the child to the phonics feature, or sound, that will be highlighted in the book. Read this page to the child, stressing the phonic feature. Help the student learn how to form the sound with her mouth. The story and engaging illustrations follow the introduction. At the end of the story, word lists categorize the feature words into their phonic elements.

Each book in this series has been carefully written to meet specific readability requirements. Close attention has been paid to elements such as word count, sentence length, and vocabulary. Readability formulas measure the ease with which the text can be read and understood. Each book in this series has been analyzed using the Spache readability formula.

Reading research suggests that systematic phonics instruction can greatly improve students' word recognition, spelling, and comprehension skills. This series assists in the teaching of phonics by providing students with important opportunities to apply their knowledge of phonics as they read words, sentences, and text.

This is the letter j.

In this book, you will read words that have the **j** sound as in: *job, jets, jacket,* and *jar.*

Jeff wishes he had a job.

Jeff's dad has a job.

He can fly big jets.

His mom is a dance teacher.

She jumps and kicks.

His brother, Jake, is a cook. He wears a special white jacket.

SAL

His sister, Jenny,
works in a shop.
She sells jars of candy.

"I wish I had a job,"

says Jeff.

"Maybe I can join the circus. I would enjoy joking around."

"I'm too young to join the circus. I would miss my family."

"We have a job for you,"
says Dad. "Your job is to
just be you!"

Fun Facts

If you want an exciting job when you grow up, consider being a wild-animal trainer. This job involves working both with animals and the public, and it requires a lot of courage! Animal trainers who work at zoos and aquariums deal with everything from dolphins to lions and tigers. This job can be dangerous, but it can also be a lot of fun. Trainers sometimes work in Hollywood if a wild animal is performing in a movie.

German scientists flew the first jet plane in 1939. Certain jets can fly at speeds greater than 760 miles (1,223 kilometers) per hour—this is faster than the speed at which sound travels! The term "jumbo jet" describes a jet that was designed to seat about 500 passengers. A pilot flew the first jumbo jet in 1970.

Activity

Just Thinking about Jobs

You have a while before you need to decide what your job will be, but you can start investigating different jobs now. If you know someone who has a job you think you might enjoy, ask if you can visit her at work one day. If you can't do that, ask her if the two of you can talk about her job. You can also visit the library and check out books about different jobs that interest you.

To Learn More

Books

About the Sound of J

Moncure, Jane Belk. *My "j" Sound Box®*. Mankato, MN: The Child's World, 2009.

About Jets

Amato, William. *Supersonic Jets*. New York: PowerKids Press, 2002.
Hill, Lee Sullivan. *Jets*. Minneapolis, MN: Lerner Publications, 2005.

About Jobs

Brooks, Felicity, and Jo Litchfield (illustrator). *Jobs People Do*. Tulsa, OK: Usborne Books, 2008.
Roberts, Carole, and Michael Garland (illustrator). *Beth's Job*. Boston: Sandpiper, 2009.

About Jokes

McCarthy, Rebecca. *Waddle Lot of Laughs*. New York: Grosset & Dunlap, 2008.
Rosenberg, Pam, and Mernie Gallagher-Cole (illustrator). *Dinosaur Jokes*. Mankato, MN: The Child's World, 2011.

Web Sites

Visit our home page for lots of links about the Sound of J:

childsworld.com/links

Note to Parents, Teachers, and Librarians: We routinely check our Web links to make sure they're safe, active sites—so encourage your readers to check them out!

J Feature Words

Proper Names

Jake
Jeff
Jenny

Feature Words in Initial Position

jacket
jar
jet
job
join
joking
jump
just

Feature Words in Medial Position

enjoy

About the Authors

Cecilia Minden, PhD, is the former director of the Language and Literacy Program at the Harvard Graduate School of Education. She is now a reading consultant for school and library publications. She earned her PhD in reading education from the University of Virginia. Cecilia and her husband, Dave Cupp, live outside Chapel Hill, North Carolina. They enjoy sharing their love of reading with their grandchildren, Chelsea and Qadir.

Joanne Meier, PhD, has worked as an elementary school teacher, university professor, and researcher. She earned her BA in early childhood education from the University of South Carolina, and her MEd and PhD in education from the University of Virginia. She currently works as a literacy consultant for schools and private organizations. Joanne lives in Virginia with her husband Eric, daughters Kella and Erin, two cats, and a gerbil.

About the Illustrator

Bob Ostrom has been illustrating children's books for nearly twenty years. A graduate of the New England School of Art & Design at Suffolk University, Bob has worked for such companies as Disney, Nickelodeon, and Cartoon Network. He lives in North Carolina with his wife Melissa and three children, Will, Charlie, and Mae.